I Am

by Mickey Daronco

Look at me.

I am a pet cat.

Am I on my mat?

Look at me.

I am a red fox.

Am I in my den?

Can you see me?

I am a hen.

Am I with my pal?

Can you see me?
I am a tan pup.
Am I with Ben?

Look up here.
I am a bug.
Am I up in a web?

Do you see me?
I am a big tan pup.
Am I in my bed?

Yes, I am.
I will have a nap.